SPEAK TO THE MOUNTAIN

So Jesus answered and said to them, "Have faith in God. For assuredly, I say to you, whoever says to this mountain, 'Be removed and be cast into the sea,' and does not doubt in his heart, but believes that those things he says will be done, he will have whatever he says. (Mark 11:22-23).

For we do not wrestle against flesh and blood, but against principalities, against powers, against the rulers of the darkness of this age, against spiritual hosts of wickedness in the heavenly places (Ephesians 6:12).

"They also will answer, 'Lord, when did we see you hungry or thirsty or a stranger or needing clothes or sick or in prison, and did not help you?' "He will reply, 'Truly I tell you, whatever you did not do for one of the least of these, you did not do for me.' "Then they will go away to eternal punishment, but the righteous to eternal life."
(Matthew25: 44-46)

The Poet's Reason Why

"When I was a boy
I did not have a talent.
When I was a boy
I made a promise to God
that if I should be given
a talent
I would use it to
its full potential.

This is why I write.

And when I write
I seek to dispel the darkness
with true light given by
the Almighty.

I am a weary traveler.
A warrior poet
with a pen like a sword
fighting for my LORD."

SPEAK TO THE MOUNTAIN

Stefon N. Lowman
Edited by Shayla R. Lowman

INk LION PRESS

SPEAK TO THE MOUNTAIN

Cover Art: by Isaac Wolf
Cover Design Idea: Lina Graphic

Paperback ISBN:978-1-7369912-0-6
ebook ISBN:978-1-7369912-1-3
Hardcover ISBN: 978-1-7369912-2-0

Printed in the United States of America

BOOK DESIGN BY STEFON N. LOWMAN

BOOK EDITED BY SHAYLA R. LOWMAN

10 9 8 7 6 5 4 3 2 1
First Paperback Edition

SPEAK TO THE MOUNTAINS

DEDICATION

This book is dedicated to Shayla, Alonna, and Lela.

TABLE OF CONTENTS

ACKNOWLEDGEMENT

THE BURNING SANDS

I remember it as if it were yesterday. In the spring of 1997, I walked into a second-floor classroom at Martin Van Buren (MVB) High School in Queens Village, NY with a few of my friends, acquaintances, and a few students I did not know. I was excited because I loved history, and this was the first opportunity that I had to take an African American History class.

For the most part, in high school I was a good student. I was always respectful to my teachers though I tried my best to fly under the radar. I always turned in my work, but I never gave 100% to my scholastic endeavors. I don't even think I knew how to give 100%. Up until that point, a teacher never challenged me to be more than just an average student. I had never been challenged to be a scholar.

On the first day of class, I sat at my desk in the back of the room making small talk with the students who sat around me. Mr. Johnson stood in front of the class. The bell rang and Mr. Johnson said something like, "In order to pass this class you will have to walk the burning sands!" "The burning sands?" I thought to myself. "What are the burning sands?" I thought as I started to panic. He continued telling us how hard we would have to work to pass his class, making it clear that this semester would be like crossing a sun-scorched desert. I envisioned myself dying in that desert with an ashen face and cracked lips. "Maybe there is still time," I thought, "still time to get out of this class." Mr. Johnson continued with a slight inflection in his voice, "You will walk the burning sands. We will all walk the burning sands together and we will get through it."

On the second day of class and the days that followed, we did not see the man that threatened us with the "Burning Sands." Instead, we encountered a man who trapped us in history and time. He taught us about our ancestors and in the process taught us about ourselves. Mr. Johnson challenged our thoughts on American History and forced us to see our place in it. We became ferocious thinkers. With each class we began to see our value as Americans, our capability as students, and our self-worth as human beings. We were growing. We were being stretched and Mr. Johnson was the catalyst. However, here is the genius of the man. He was not stretching us, instead he was inspiring us, and we were stretching ourselves. In his class, we became scholastic Bedouin. Without knowing it we had been crossing the burning sands. We accepted the rigor of the course with excitement because we had been inspired.

A small spark of inspiration can start a wildfire, and

once started it is difficult to put out. There are so many stories that I could tell about how Mr. Johnson inspired us to be more than what we thought we were or could be. I could tell you about the time he sent us to the Jamaica Queens library on the weekend to do a research project, then followed up a few weeks later by sending us to The Museum of Modern Art (MoMA), on the weekend for another research project to observe African American art. We were inner city kids mainly from Northside and Southside Jamaica (Southeast Queens) and I get the sense that the papers that we wrote were not the learning objective, but vehicles for us to be exposed to a different environment. It was all about inspiring us, and if inspiration was his goal he succeeded greatly.

With aiming to inspire, Mr. Johnson changed my life. One day in class we read *Mother to Son* by Langston Hughes. I expressed to Mr. Johnson how the poem spoke to me. Mr. Johnson responded by telling me that I was going to write a ballad for homework. "I don't write no ballads," I responded without thinking. You see I was from around the way, and a kid from around the way did not write ballads. Mr. Johnson responded in a calm manner, "You will if you want to pass this class," and that was that. Later that night I struggled at my dining room table to write a ballad; internally I was walking the burning sands. Although Mr. Johnson always insinuated that walking the burning sands would be painful, he also let us know that it was profitable. And it was. By the end of the night, I had my ballad, and I was proud of it. Something broke inside this city kid. Beneath the concrete that lined my soul was fertile ground of inspired thought and words to be used to weave them together. Because of Mr. Johnson I discovered that I had a skill for writing poetry. From that point on, I wrote myself out of mediocrity.

Two years later while in college at Florida A&M University the talent that Mr. Johnson helped me to discover, led me to change my major to Journalism and Public Relations and inspired me to create and become the editor of a poetry and art section in my college newspaper called the Creative Mindz. I also became a staff writer in my school newspaper and lived history as a beat reporter during the 2000 elections. Like a snowball effect this passion that Mr. Johnson sparked, led me to my first job at HBO in marketing (since public relation was an easy transition to marketing), and every career decision that I made in my life, ultimately leading me to become a Lead Counselor at a middle school in North Carolina. I wanted to impact the future like Mr. Johnson did. However, through all this time I never stopped writing poetry. It became my passion.

In 2019, I self-published a poetry book titled, *A Million and One Stories to Tell.* During the process I thought of Mr.

Johnson often and the burning sands. Once the book was released on Amazon, I wanted to find him to show him how he inspired me in my life. I wanted to show him the end result of his work as an educator. After reaching out to some great people I found him. When I got him on the phone, I intended to share with him how he impacted my life. My goal was to pay it forward and in turn impact his life. However, he proceeded to question me about being an educator and asked me what I thought about the current world we live in and how I could influence students as an educator. He also inspired me as a writer and helped me gain inspiration for this current book that I had been struggling with. Just as in the past, over a few short conversations over the phone he helped me to focus on the current events happening in our world. This was at the beginning of the Covid-19 lockdown. For me this was a short trip through the burning sand because I did not want to focus on these events, but the murder of George Floyd changed everything. I plan to send him an advance copy of this book. Mr. Johnson is a remarkable man who encounters students and turns them into desert dwellers who are fully equipped to walk the burning sands of this life. We were never students to Mr. Johnson. He always saw us as scholars, scholastic Bedouins.

—Stefon N. Lowman, The Publisher

PREFACE

In my heart, I am a revolutionary. I have always hoped that I would become an agent of change. I believe in change for the betterment so long as the change is based on truth and truth comes from The Most-High. This book attempts to evoke change in the place where it matters most, the inner chambers of the soul. Changing its trajectory from the lie to the truth.

Speak to The Mountain is a book of poetry meant to be read from cover to cover, from beginning to end in order for the thematic message to be understood. Thematically this book picks up where my previous book, *A Million and One Stories To Tell* left off. Rather than focusing on stories, this book focuses on theme. Although, Babylon fell at the end of my previous book the more sinister mountains remain, and like Babylon are animated by the same evil beings. Each poem builds upon one another to make up a thematic whole. The theme of the book is speaking truth to power. The metaphor of the mountain depicts powerful dark forces in our world, such as systemic racism and the more sinister spiritual forces of Satan and his kingdom that animate the evil of the material world. Initially, when I endeavored to write this book I wanted to focus on the many dark forces (mountains) that presents itself and blocks people's path in life. However, because of the Covid-19 lockdown and the events that followed the murder of George Floyd the only mountain that I could see while writing was the mountain of racism. The particular racism that we deal with within the United States presents itself as a mighty mountain, one that crushes both the oppressor and the oppressed. It is so deep-rooted that it seems to pierce through the physical world into the realm of the soul, and that is exactly where I believe racism gains its power. Unlike a disease that can be treated with medicines or herbs, racism is a disease of the soul. The end goal of racism is the total destruction of that which is different than one's self. It is the destruction of a human being in every area of life including the right to be human, but even more so the right to be a being. A being is far higher than an animal. A being is sentient and has a special connection with God, The Most High. Therefore, the human being is in company with the cherubim, seraphim, and other spiritual beings in God's divine council. All standing in the presence of God, but also, unfortunately, sentients is also shared with the fallen heavenly beings as well. They are opposed to human beings having the right of being sentient beings. This is the eternal right that God offered to all human beings. Racism attempts to nullify that right by dragging the human being to a place below the animal. Racism invades all social systems and uses those systems to oppress and crush. The ironic thing is that it is based on a lie. Race is a social construct used to subjugate people of darker pigmentation.

   This leads us to the African who for the better part of 400 years has borne the brunt of the heavyweight of Racism. In this book, I attempted to make the case that racism is conceived in the spiritual world, birthed in the soul, and through human beings manifests itself as an all-encompassing force in our physical world. Since it started in the spiritual world it can only be defeated in the spiritual world, and this is the setting of the book. With the help of three archetypical figures; The African, The Stranger, and The Poet; the reader is taken on a journey of healing and reconciliation.

—Stefon N. Lowman, The Publisher

THE WAR (THE POET'S PROLOGE)

The battle rages
all logic
        and reason
would state
that we
are at a disadvantage,
void of understanding
with weak knees
supposedly deceived–
denying reality,
but we
walk by faith
and not by sight.

Therefore, we march fighting–
in the darkest night.
Conventional wisdom states
that we should be blind,
engulfed in perpetual darkness
like a black moon eclipsing the sun.
However, rash conclusions
such as these would be foolish
because conventional wisdom is often wrong.

In denial and refusing
to be cast away
our enemy surrounds us.
Cloaked in a lie
they try
to smother us.

I wish that they were all
cast down to hell
when Babylon fell
instead of down to the dust
to war with us.

To the deceived eye
we are a breath
away
from defeat,
but we
see past the physical;
we don't have a third eye
because that
is a lie.
Rather we are indwelled by the Spirit
of the most-high;

the Ruach HaKodesh
which enables us to see into the spiritual
that true reality;
our native land
full of light
and sanctity.

The darkness is surrounded
and already defeated
for this reason
we claim victory.
We see past time and space.
Past the grave
and we
behold life.

We embrace truth
in the spiritual
and hurl it at the physical
shattering lies.
Shards of glass
like knives
impale our enemies.

Demons, imps, giants,
and satan himself flee
from our God
shinning above
casting down shadows
that fall beneath
our feet.

SONGS OF FREEDOM

The African [stressed th ee; unstressed before a consonant th uh; unstressed before a vowel th ee] [af-ri-kuh n]

Noun

1. One who sings and dances before mountains until they come crashing down.
2. Stolen people. Betrayed people. Diaspora.
3. One without tribe and nation of origin. Therefore, embraces the continent.
4. A resilient being, fearfully and wonderfully made.
5. An indestructible spirit loved by The King.

MAREJESHO (RESTORATION)

Stolen from Africa.
Son of Trinidadian & Vincentian;
African Caribbean.
Born in Brooklyn
raised in Jamaica, New York;
north—
in the Village of Queens;
south—
among African Caribbeans;
children of Africa.

Eyes have never seen the continent
from which my blackness came.
Brownskin seeks to
teach
the truth lost to European colonialism
and systemic racism.

I want to stare in the eyes
of my brothers
across the sea
restore a family line
broken
by centuries
of lies.

Maybe the continental African
can help me find
the tribe
that birthed me.
I yearn for home—
to restore

identity.

Make me into a whole man.
Allow me to take
my place
with the African.
Diaspora restored—
to tribe and nation.

Nations united!

As one continent
let us exorcise the ghost
of colonialism
and enslavers;
breaking the chains
of the European
to be
culturally free.

Physically
made whole
to stand strong
among the nations
as human beings.

DIVIDED

Imaginary labels
created to divide.
A social construct
with aims to deconstruct
humanity.
Souls are categorized
by shells of dust
meant to walk the earth
and subject to decay.
Meant to live and love,
but caused to hate,
kill, exploit, and enslave.
Caused to live in suspicion
never trusting
never understanding
never changing.
Forever at war.

The creator's rose garden is complete
with every hue
that light can conceive
with every electromagnetic
radiated beam that the eye
can see.
Roses clothed
by visual perception
along a spectrum
divided and separated
and we call
it
race;
a social construct,

a figment of our imagination.

But if race does not exist
then why do we
continue to invoke
its name
and use it to marginalize our children?
Use it as a Likert scale
for intelligence,
and wage war
in institutions?

Once the justification for colonialism,
the MAAFA,
and eugenics,
but currently used to maintain the
status quo
a caste system destroying souls
of light and darker
shades alike,
as we remain fixed.
Humanity lost
in this
matrix.

Nigger

Moor
  Negro
Colored Folk
Black
Afro American
African American
Afro Latino
African Caribbean

I travel through history
searching
for truer identity.
One not defined
by slavery.

I travel through time
and simultaneously across
the Atlantic
to be greeted
by my face
as

The African

WE; THE AFRICAN

We claim the name
of our ancestral birth.
We like Joseph
have been sold
by our brothers
into slavery
for gold, for guns, recognition;
dreams of wealth
on the Gold Coast.

We, carried across
the sea.
Broken
into pieces
by our captors
and scattered
like dust over the Americas.
Chained,
enslaved,
bought,
sold.
Born and died
on plantations.
Buried.

We, darkened seeds
spread across
southern states,
the Caribbean,
Brazil,
blending with indigenous people
and enslavers

conquering the blood
becoming King
of genes.
We, seeds
bring forth roots
in the soil
of our new home.
Desire for freedom
sprouts like green leaves
reaching
towards heaven.
Flowers bear fruit
native to the mother
continent beyond the sea.
Though
identity
stolen,
the soul never
forgets.
Memories travel
across the sea.
The hurricane
and
the desert wind
begs us to never forget,
yells for us
to wake
up,
and beckons that we remember
who
we
are.

Brown eyes lids
open.
Chains
broken.
Diaspora
awoken.

Memorandum to the African Diaspora

To: The stolen children of Africa
From: The Poet
Date: Backdated 6/19/1865
          Documented 6/19/2020

- There is no such thing as a free slave

- If you allow yourself to be called a slave after freedom you will forever be a slave without chains

- You should never be called a slave because you were not created as a slave. Replace slave with enslaved

- Your history does not begin with chains and enslavement

- Teach your children this before they are miseducated by the educational system

- You are not a slave

TRAPPED IN THOUGHT

Sometimes I;
The African
sit and ponder
unsearchable things;
deep matters
of the human soul
like how a black man
can sell out his own
for pieces of gold,
how a white Evangelical
could hate his own Christian brother
because of the color
of his skin,
and how the Black Panther Party
was targeted by the FBI,
yet the KKK
is allowed to remain
unchanged.

DREAMWALKER

Last night
I had a dream.
I was in chains.
Captured by a pirate
named Lowman
planted on a sugar plantation
in Chateaubelair.
Enslaved
on a tiny island
that in the waking world
my feet have never touched.
My eyes gaze
at the Caribbean Sea
and towards
the Grenadines.

Paradise quickly
turned to hell
by the whip
at my back.
Flesh split open
blood trickles
from
back
to glutes
to hamstring
to ankle
to Vincentian soil.

If only
I could grow
a new me

from blood
like seeds
and that man
would be free.

Instead, I toil
in chains
on a British colony.
Bound in an
ancestorial dream.

THE AFRICAN

L ife has tried to beat
him down and grind him
into dust,
but
he keeps on
getting
up.

The Young Black Masculine Face in the Instructional Space

My third-grade teacher hated me.
Acted maliciously.
Tried to destroy me.
She used the education system
as a weapon.
to demolish my confidence
and my ability to dream.

She tried to discourage me
and trick me
by luring me
into the school
to
prison
pipeline,
but she failed.
I defeated her
with a master's degree.

Woe to those
who crush seeds
under their feet
before they become trees.
They should be condemned
to walk in shame
laden with chains
for giving teachers
a bad name
as well as those who save the youth;

especially the darker than blue
who grow into men
with voices baritone.
They reach for tomorrow
not for steel bars.
They reach
only for freedom.

BE FARMERS

Plant the seeds
and let them grow.
What they'll become
you do not know.
They may be trees
so tend to the weeds.
Let them breathe
give them water
they may even become something
greater
only found in dreams.

THE CITY KID

These are the ingredients:
Eastern Parkway,
Bedford Stuyvesant,
and Crown Heights.
A dash of Brownsville,
a pinch of Flatbush,
and a few slices of Canarsie.

A Roti, a hamburger, and beef patty.
Blend well,
bake under the heat
of life,
chill on the cold concrete
and you'll have...

Kyeem; the city kid
who chased a dream
only to succeed.
He defeated the streets
when it was ruled by Babylon.
Saw friends fall
to the grave.
Lost others in penitentiaries enslaved,
but guided by a dream
he tackled destiny
and put fate in a headlock.
In 90's fashion
he snuffed the stereotypes
of what a young black teen was supposed to be.
He sent them scattering,
babbling,
and back to the throats

of those who fail to believe
that a kid from the streets
could make it
to the University
without a ball in his hand
then return to the land
of kings
as a man and
as a beacon of hope
for lost seeds
trapped in the clutches
of a malicious system
and share the full recipe
of the plan to defeat it.

BROWN MAN BLACK SHADOWS

B lack like outer darkness
or black like the skin of the African?
But my skin is not black
it is brown
like the dust from which I was created;
as Adam,
as Eve,
as human being.

But what is in a name,
and why do you really
call me black?

Do you envision a void
in place of a soul?
Or is it black
like death;
an impending extinction event,
or maybe black like nightmare?
Why am I the embodiment
of what your conscience
causes you to fear?

In your mind does black
make us like demons;
like incubus and succubus?
Is that why you wish us
vanquished,
and if so by which tool?
Is it with the gun,
the knee, or the noose?

Do you fear black magic
because you fear
the so-called black man?

But my skin is not black
it is brown
like the dust of the ground
which brings forth life,
beauty, and the crown
jewel
of God's creation.

TO THE WHITE SUPREMACIST CHRISTIAN

Dear Christian,

What if you discovered
that Jesus' skin was brown?
Would you cease to follow him,
throwing your cross to the ground?
Would you become like Judas?
Would you justify
the actions
of Pontius Pilate?

And after the third day—
Jesus in his glorious body;
seeing his skin
still brown, but radiant like bronze,
would you still
want to go to heaven?
or
would you reject him?

And what if satan
appeared
out of luminous light
as a man whose skin
is White.
Would you choose
to follow him?

Would your hatred and pride
cause you
to cast eternity aside

to serve a god
of your own kind
just so you
could feel right
and reign supreme
with him
in the lake
of fire?

THE SYSTEM

Broken systems
like broken dreams.

Broken systems
like cyanide-laced streams.

Broken systems
like broken promises
corralling the masses
into mental incarceration.

MY COUNTRY?

My country tis of thee sweet land of liberty?

Land of the free
home of the brave.

This is America;
hand in pocket
adding pressure to the leg
of knees bent
crushing the neck
of those
it was sworn to protect.

This is America burning.
Voices lifted up like
flames;
the cries of the enslaved.
The privileged forced to listen
through an inferno
of their own making.

This is America;
boasting of freedom
and equity,
while using dishonest scales,
kicking black babies
as they crawl,
tripping black boys
as they run,
interrupting black men
in their prime
ending their lives with the gun.

This is America;
destroyer of those
of African descent.
Architect of institutional racism
saboteur of souls.

America;
propagator of false dreams.

Land of the free
home of the brave,
but not for those
like me.

LAST BREATH

I can't breathe!
Officer, officer
please take your
knee off me!
Officer, officer
please stop
choking me!

Sir? Ma'am? Teacher?
Can I be treated
equally?
I want to learn,
but I can't breathe.
The walls are closing
in on me.
I am being placed behind bars,
but I just want
to thrive.

I want to reach the stars
and see the Milky Way,
but I am choking on thin air.
I can't breathe,
I can't breathe.
Officer, officer,
I can't...

BURNING CITIES

These flames are old
flames.
It really isn't fire
at all.
It is blood rising
up
crying out
begging to be heard.
Clawing up walls.
Climbing over buildings
screaming for vengeance
administered
by The King.

A brother's blood
spilled
by his next of kin.
Murdered by him,
who should have been his keeper,
but abdicated
because of the color of his skin.

Now the cities
burn
as retribution for his sin.

A VISION OF HEAVEN ON EARTH

I dream of heaven
and no racist police officers are trying to keep me out.
I dream of heaven,
where all black people are proud to be called African,
singing praises to God
while he blesses them.
In this heaven,
love is everlasting.
Racism, hate, and pride
are things of the past
cast into hell with satan.

And this is heaven
because the Native Americans are the only Americans.
They are safe
and never go hungry
because the Buffaloes still
roam free
grazing by the millions
along western plains.

In my heaven
slave ships never sailed to African shores,
and China never had to
open its doors.
There were no cotton farms
and the world never knew
of world wars or atom bombs.

In heaven
I see Amadou Diallo

sitting with Malcolm
and Martin
making plans to visit Lumumba
and they gather with many others
to teach our children
who grow to love themselves.

So, it is all good brotha man.
Peace sista girl.
We are safe
and there is love
because this
is heaven.

CHANT OF THE AFRICAN

America has killed
the best of us.

So now America is left
with the rest of us,
and we
won't
be victims
anymore.

We are human beings,
and by faith
declare ourselves
free.

INVITATION FOR GROWTH

Like dew
in the morning
are words
traveling
over great distances
from the lips
of a stranger.

Alluring
and calling
for The African
to follow
to come forth
to grow.

WHO IS HE?

After
culture is restored
and the result of theft
has been abated,
introspection
leads to a question:
Who can restore
the soul?

Culture can't
achieve this feat.
The natural
cannot change
the spiritual being.

As the colonizer
tore down
cultural identity
and attempted
to crush broken pieces
under his feet,
The enemy
of all souls
stole life
warping and twisting
spiritual beings
clothed with humanity.

Eternity lost,
but like cultural identity
paradise can be found again
so, the question remains:
Who can restore
the soul?

BROKEN PIECES OF GOLD

The Stranger [stressed th ee; unstressed before a consonant th uh; unstressed before a vowel th ee] [streyn-jer]

Noun

1. Perhaps a prophet or an angel, but always a messenger sent from God bringing hope that collapses stone bringing mountains down.
2. One who rescues from despair.
3. Servent of The King.

THE BOND SERVANT

I am a stranger to most.
A follower of One.
A restorer of men.
I am a weary traveler traversing the road of life.
I have walked through cities
and beautiful country sides.

My feet have stepped in puddles in dark alleyways
and through streams
overshadowed by beautiful mountain ranges.

I have seen the beauty of the full moon
accompanied by stars illuminating night,
and I have been scorched by the sun burning the clouds
that refused to share the sky.

I have seen spring turn to fall
and watched as winter
covers all.

I have observed the world turn to ice
only to submit to time
and bring forth life.

Sojourner that I am
I have observed this world
and the ways of man.
Behind it all,
as my feet press against the cobblestone
I can vaguely see
in the horizon
the hand of the almighty controlling

it all,
and it warms my heart
so I fix my gaze
on my road again
traveling as a stranger
to uplift the hearts of men.

THE GOATS & THE WHITE SUPREMACIST CHRISTIAN

"I was a stranger and you did not invite me in."

Dear Christian,
You are supposed
to be my brother,
but you left me
in chains robbed,
naked, and beaten
on the road.

I thought we followed
the same master
and in turn
I thought you were
to me a neighbor,
but you passed me by
and even conspired
with my assailant
through your ambivalence.

You refused
to help me
though
we are supposed to be
brothers.
You treated me
like a stranger.
You became like Cain
and I became
like Abel to you.

You poured salt
on my open wound.
You kicked me
as I lay, with outstretched arms
bleeding
along the cobblestone road.
You gave me no grace
as I lay helpless on the ground.
You showed me no mercy
just because my skin is brown.

THE BROKEN THINGS

God searches for
the broken things,
the discarded pieces
and fastens them together.

He makes them beautiful and
whole again.

The hands that created the universe
makes all things new.

BEAUTIFUL BROWN SKIN

Don't believe the lie
sunshine
The dark clouds are not powerful
enough to snatch you
out of the sky.

On rainy days
it is hard for her to
keep the pain away
because it is trapped inside
hiding from her emotions.
With a weaving motion
she slices the skin
attempting to feel again.
Listening,
to the voice in her head
telling her that she is worthless,
her life meaningless,
and would be better breathless.
But those words are lies;
fabrications.

You are beautiful, sunshine.
One of a kind,
and your future is bright;
luminous, glorious, and radiant
putting the stars to shame,
and God knows your name.
He formed you with his hands.
A unique creation.
A monumental achievement
for the creator of everything.

Beautiful skin
not made for razors
and other sharpened things.

Just as beautiful skin
was not made for whips
scarring backs,
ropes that burn and break necks,
or chains that bind the wrist.
Your life matters.
You matter.

Don't believe the lie
sunshine.
The dark clouds are not powerful
enough to snatch you
out of the sky.

THE STRANGER AND THE YOUNG AFRICAN

Listen, to my voice
it may sound strange.
Truth often
feels foreign to one coming
out of caves.

You are not a thug.
You are a soldier!
A revolutionary.
On your feet
mighty warrior
shake the dust from your brown skin.
Leave the street corner behind
and join the tribe of The African.

Listen, let this stranger
teach you
who
you
are.

You were made
in the image
of God.

Your brown skin
a dim reflection
of his
bronze.

THE MAKER

Did you know
that God
was intentional
when he made you.

The one
who crafted
the rose
was the one
who formed
your nose,
and with his
fingertips
He carved out
your lips.

With great joy
He wrapped you
in your brown skin.
Then he blew his life
into you
and you became a living being.
He gave you
beauty
as your
glory.
He made you
free.

BECOME

Take my hand,
        says
                The Stranger,
as he lifts The African
to his feet.

Take your place
among the nations.
Let none look down
on you anymore.

Eye to eye.
Soul to soul.
Spirit to spirit.

All human beings
waiting to be
set free.

MOUNTAINS

Mountains are peculiar beings.
They divide kingdoms.
They are built
with jagged stones
of oppression, racism,
division, and rebellion.
They tower from
earth to heaven
carrying the unmistakable
stench
of a serpent,
angering The King.

FALSE CHRISTIAN

Woe to you!
You can't make a disciple
with a gun.
A whip is a useless tool
to redeem
souls.

Negating the scriptures
and dehumanizing
a continent
won't bring you closer to God.

False Christian;
like
fool's
gold.
More visible than the real thing,
but is found unworthy in purifying heat.
Left as coal; brittle and dust like
blown away in the wind.

You
teach the world
to hate
the true and living God.
Ignorant of who you are
they believe you
represent Christ.

You who are void of the Ruach HaKodesh.

You hypocrites
who hate your brother,
but claim you love
God
because you think
he is just like you.

You who fail to read
the scriptures you tote.
Ignorant of the word
you murder your neighbor.
You fail to care for
the least of these.
Woe to you,
you hypocrites.
You political Christians.
You racists.
How dare you call yourself Christian.

For as you have done
to the least of these
you have done
to Jesus
and He
in His glory
is not pleased.

THE MESSENGER

The Stranger
is cloaked in mystery.
Face hooded
like a monk.
Voice bellowing
like the seraphim;
mighty
messenger of God.
Words spoken
with authority.
Syntax
wakes
the dead.

African, Asian, European,
Native American, and all
human beings
all spiritually dead.
All sinners
in need of a savior
who became a King.

THE MESSAGE

The Stranger
came bellowing
speaking words
that some claim
new,
but The Stranger speaks
an old message
meant for all human
beings
not just for the Europeans.

Imperialists attempted
to hijack it,
weaponize it,
and make it their own,
but The King sent
The Stranger
to rescue it from the supremacist
and the self-righteous
in order to present it to
the world.

Every culture,
every tribe
follow The Stanger
as he leads you
to the One
who
restores
the
soul.

GOD'S WORK

A stranger could be a friend to those seeking
to be free-
like The African
a strange dichotomy.

Never see?
Come see.

The stranger is
a herald
speaking words
that make darkness flee
as truth causes
lies to collapse.

A lamp for the feet.
A light for the path.

Darkness tries to react,
but victory stands beyond its grasp.
But only if we stand in the light;
illuminated in truth
and the darkness
can't comprehend this.

This is the way
walk in it.
A luminous path
that leads
to life.
May our footsteps be guided
by The Stranger's staff.

INVITATION TO FREEDOM

The darkness
    of this world
has become commonplace,
so truth,
comes as a stranger.

The Stranger says
come!

Come, to
The African,
The Asian,
The Arab, and
The European!

Come,
let us reconcile
and destroy the fruits
of imperialism.

All ethnic groups
upon the earth,
come!

To The Native American
and all their
tribes
come!

Come!
Let us find freedom.

FREEDOM'S JOURNEY

The Poet
followed The Stranger and The African
as they traveled across the sea;
across the Atlantic
for reconciliation
and something more
only found
in dreams.

GOD, MEN, ANGELS, THE WAR, AND PRINCIPALITIES & POWERS

The Poet [stressed th ee; unstressed before a consonant th uh; unstressed before a vowel th ee] [poh-it]

Noun

1. Inspired by God, crafter of words; spiritual weapons that tear down strongholds, destroyer of mighty mountains.
2. A warrior wielding a pen in service to The King.
3. One who has faith.

Head in The Clouds

Why not now,
Poet?
Why not write
a song now
and wrap it
around the
wind,
harness it gently,
loop it like
the needle to the string?
Declare it to the
heavens
with the ink of a pen.

So why not proclaim,
Poet?
Exclaim as The African
finds his place
among the nations.
Though voices
have been silent
for quite
sometime
why not contribute now?
Join in while the angels
are singing psalms
to YHWH
as He listens with
open ears.

The Poet has written a song
that should be bellowed

to the clouds.
So why not sing it now
young African
 while youth is in your grasp?
While Yahweh smiles
on all creation
and holds them in
His hands.

The Poet's Revelation

Enough is enough.
Where is the love?
So much injustice.
Where is God?

I can't stay here
down in the dust.
LORD help me
rise above.

I must speak
to the mountain,
and the
mountain is spiritual.

It is said that
racism and injustice
are the handiwork
of spiritual beings,
and we
human beings
are deceived
by principalities.

Culture against culture
and
kingdom against kingdom.
While we wrestle
they have trapped us in Babylon
again.

In Babylon, we are walled in

by many mountains,
and we are all blinded by darkness
and indignation.

But I can't stay here.

I must
prepare
for war.

DECLARATION OF WAR

Wake up African,
          says The Stranger.
And through your faith and prayers
be changed
to an indestructible being.
The LORD
has set you free.

Come near Poet,
          says The Stranger,
and become a scribe
of the
indescribable
in the service
of The King.

The day of maturity has come.
We must
tear down the mountain.

THE POET & THE GRIOT

The Poet followed The African
led by The Stranger
to The African's native land
for reconciliation.
The Poet saw mountains come down
one by one
from
Lamban
and the song
that The Griot
sung.

The African
is greeted by
the West African drum.
Native and Diaspora
dance in celebration
joined as one
nation.
The Poet meets The Griot
and crafts
psalms
to the melody
of the kora
and balafon.
History restored
by The Griot's poem.
Then The Stranger leads all
arm in arm
as one family
in the direction of The King
prepared as warriors

armed
and restored to
join with the nations
on a path parched
through the enemy's
abode of burning sands
and
perilous times.

The only road
to rest.

Perilous Times

Self-centeredness
the norm.
This generation
deformed.
They stare at the clouds,
but don't
anticipate the storm.

THE UPSIDE-DOWN WORLD

All I see is chaos and confusion.
Mirages and illusions.
False light
from a false god
in search of an adopted son
with hopes to claim deity
and be like the I AM.

Hoping to rule beings
devolved into beasts
void of wisdom
and understanding
creating a future
made in the image of that false god;
that fallen angel.

Rebels full of pride
are completely blind.
These are they who turned the world
upside down
where a cherub can proclaim himself god.

Now sit tight and don't move.
Prepare for madness;
bacchanal and
insanity running rampant,
ignorance defended,
everyone offended,
death embraced.
Fallen angels and carbon-based sentient beings alike

grasping for heaven,
but only finding
darkness and eternal flames.

SHUJAA (WARRIOR)

Traveling with The African (the Diaspora)
and their native kin
on a pilgrimage
to The King
led by The Stranger.

Brown bodies gather
into a large aggregation
to battle
against the mountain.
Men and women
changed into
Warrior Poets
and Shujaa Groits
in the service of The King.

Truthful words
are like swords
on tongues.
Each swipe
like light
making darkness run.

THE REAL ENEMY

Behind the eyes
of every racist cop
and each xenophobic politian
you were there.

In the mouth of every
racist teacher
I heard your voice.

It was your idea to divide
the human race.
You used The European
as your tool
and set God's creation
against each other
based on a lie
called race
and the horrors of imperialism,
slavery, and genocide.

You, son of the morning.
The rebel of heaven
sought to destroy everything.

Now let us stones cry out
and unite against him.
Warriors from every
nation, culture, and creed.

Let Christ's body
wake up and take

to the heavens
to tear your kingdom down.

THE PRINCIPALITIES AND POWERS

Like marauders at midnight
they came out
of the sky
cloaked in the darkness
of night
whispering lies
in an attempt to steal
my will to fight.

These beings;
hordes
of the enemy
accosted me
when I became
spiritually fatigued.

You see the burning sands
are a vast sea
of uncertainty
stealing hope and the will
of the fearful and weak.
Even strong men
buckle
to their knees.
The horizon offers
no peace
only the immovable mountain
challenging all who believe.

It was when we stopped for the night
and The African and The Stanger were asleep
that I meet the principalities.

We wrestled all night as they attempted
to steal my vision
of The King,
kill my hopes and dreams,
and destroy my soul;
the most important part of me.
Overwhelmed,
I contemplated
and considered
giving in to defeat.

How can a man fight the invisible?

Then suddenly,
I saw angels
illuminating the night.
I saw the war
and darkness trying to resist,
but ultimately fleeing before the light.

With my tormentors gone
angelic beings
kept watch
over me and impressed
upon me
to rest.
My soul
spent
and I wondered
where my faith
and confidence went.
Drifting into sleep I pray
and yearn
for the day.

LIVE!

Just after the falling of the dew,
The Poet
sat down
on a rock exhausted and dejected
beside The African.
Acknowledging each other
they both sat staring
at the vastness of
the burning sands.
They sat in silence
for what felt like an eon,
but
it was only a moment.

Then The Poet said:
  It is no use.
  The sand
  spans
  for miles
  from horizon
  to horizon
  and in the distance
  the mountain
  climbs
  to
  high.
  Its top pierces the sky.
  Its summit reaching
  heaven,
  but shows no reverence,
  and it is too wide.

Its width
is not measured in miles,
but in time.
Ages would pass
and
one would die
trying to go around its expanse.

The world is sand
and mountain.
All I see is EVIL.

Before The African
could respond
The Stranger appeared
hearing every word
The Poet said.
Sitting between them both
and explained:

EVIL is only life
corrupted.
The absence
of a preservative.

A small amount of salt
preserves meat.
As a tiny bit of light
can force darkness
to flee.

Consider this:

Let yourself not be troubled.
You are stronger than you think.
It is important to remember
the One who empowers
as you traverse these shifting sands.
He won't let you sink.
Villainy and treachery,
  though giants,
  are foolish things
  often their ostentatious displays
  fail
  at the faith of tiny beings.
Eventually
the rebellious,
the heinous,
the destructive,
the iniquitous,
the atrocious,
the malicious,
and the vile
crumble
and become woeful things
crushed by the unadulterated hands
of The King.

You see, The Stranger said,
we must walk the burning sands
because in us
is victory.
EVIL carries within it
its defeat

and that fact,
that truth
commands us to LIVE!
At that,
The Poet, The African, and The Stranger
stood up
from the stone
and continued their path
on the burning
sands
determined to get beyond
the mountain
to The King's Throne.

THE SERPENT AND THE TRUTH

There can only
be
one liar.

The serpent tells
conflicting tales
consisting of
prepositions,
nouns,
boastful words,
and verbs
meant to
move souls from
the truth.

Venom is a sentence
concealed
mysteriously
returning to remembrance
when least expected
to do the most damage.

Ah, the truth,
and there is only One
having talons
of a great eagle
breaking bones
squeezing the life
out of the lie.

THE MASQUERADERS AND THEIR SLAVES

Heaven,
only the brave in spirit live here;
those who have the courage
to turn their backs
on this world's system
built by men
empowered by satan
and all fallen angels
who dwell in a false heaven,
below the real invisible heaven,
crudely copied;
into a twisted version
in our visible space.
The temporary dwelling place
of the rebels
until that future date
when it is cast down to the pit,
but for now those spiritual beings dwell above the clouds
occasionally coming down, but
they
are
not
gods.

They are not God.

They are the enemies of the soul,
Babylon's architects and the fathers and
the embodiment of Midnight.
They are cosmic hypocrites,
monsters of the deep blue sea,

mirages in a transient desert
confined by time and human minds
taking on the mantles of deities
to hide
their predatory schemes.

They want to destroy you—
mesmerize you with human wisdom,
and initiate some with magic,
which originated from them,
while granting your every desire, but
false in nature
designed to distract
until the body dies.
Leaving an empty soul
and a spirit lifeless and unfit for eternity
like dried up flowers
meant for a beautiful garden,
but now only fit to be uprooted
and burned.

Spiritual cowards
now only suitable to be inhabitants
of hell.

PEOPLE LIKE TREES

This dark place
void of hope
is where faith begins
because there is One
who transcends the
darkness
and heals the blind
restoring sight
returning them to the light.

In a Name

I know fear
and it has a name,
but why speak it
and give power to the darkness.

I know fear,
but I know one
greater.
he has a name
and I will speak it.
No, I will scream it
because in Yeshua Hamashiach
There is power
to destroy
the darkness.

THE WAY TO THE KING

Few find it.
Many grow
weary.
Most give up
on the narrow cobblestone.
Many choose to follow
the broad
yellow bricked road
laden with glitter and gold,
but that way does not
lead to The King,
only to false destinations
in broken dreams;
destruction
as far as the eyes can see.

Few find it,
and those that do march
in a single filed line
with eyes
fixed forward.
Narrow is the road
no room
for heavy baggage.
This is light infantry.
Soldiers walk the steep path
that lead
to the feet
of
The King.

THE KING AND HIS SERVANTS

Heaven,
only the brave in spirit live here;
those who have the courage
to turn their back
on this world's system
and follow The King
who gave his life
and took it up again
for the reconciliation
of the human spirit.

IN THE GARDEN

A foot was made for stomping
in the garden.
A heel was meant for grinding
the head of the serpent.

Don't let him speak.

With toenails
tear his body.
Mutilate his flesh
and eliminate the lie.
The forked tongue wants to control you
own you
lure you into slavery
that lasts for eternity,
but forceful feet could stop his scheme
and destroy the ophidian.

THE KING'S ARMY

Speak the name of The King.
Speak it to the mountain
and watch it fall.
Speak it to the dry bones
and watch marrow
stirring,
flesh growing,
and an army rising
out of the sand.
Witness the reinforcements
of the warrior
poet
at war against the darkness.

THE WORD

Standing on Mars Hill
crying out to the unknown God
who is above all.
He spoke His word
and it became a sword.
God changes men into foot soldiers;
dry bones into battalions.
Squadrons facing the bellowing
of the serpent
who thinks himself a lion
whose army is fear
and darkness.
Our only weapon is the sword.
This sword
killed the roaring lion,
impaled the serpent,
and cut off the head of the dragon.
The sword made the darkness flee,
so we point it at the mountains
believing that they will
fall into the sea.

THE ONE WHO SPEAKS TO THE MOUNTAIN

All giants
fall
down.
The great ones,
the arrogant,
the copious,
the malicious,
and the magical.

They all fall
at the feet of the small
and despised ones who trust
in One greater than the mountain
only to watch those rocky
bodies
crumble.
Humbled
by words of courage
spoken from the lips
of one who believes
and written
with the sword
of The
Poet
in honor
of The King.

SPEAK TO THE MOUNTAIN

At the foot of the mountain
we stood
as we are joined
by the nations.

The African and their kin
made nodding
gestures
to The Asian,
The Hebrew,
The Native
American,
The Arab,
The European,
and all others.
There as one creation.

Everyone
carried
their
own
lamp.

To think
we almost did not make it.

      The desert sands
      and the howling wind
      buffeted us
      along the way.
      Each grain
      sliced at our cheeks

like shards of glass
in efforts to dissuade.
The wind attempted to bury us
in the desert.
But by God's grace
we made it.
The African and The Stranger
grabbed each of my hands
and pulled me out
of the burning sands.

Now we stand
at the foot of the mountain
looking up
as its summit disappeared
into the clouds
and we stood amazed
as a figure clothed in light appeared
as if stepping out of heaven
all ablaze.
The African and his kin
looked up hopefully.
Hoping to meet
The King.

His light was blinding,
radiant
like a thousand suns.
So bright
that our lamps
and vision

darkened.
Then he began to sing
the most beautiful melody;
spellbinding
putting our souls
to sleep.
I overheard The European
saying,
this must be The King
and the others agreed.
When he stopped singing
there was silence
and adoration.

The desert wind blew gently.

Then the one clothed in light
smiled like
a conquering hero
standing before us majestically.
Then he began
to speak.

He greeted
The African
and
The European
then all human beings.
His words
were mesmerizing
causing some to fall

to their knees.
Then he beckoned us
to worship
and swear allegiance to
him.

It was then
that The Stranger
caught my eye.

In a commanding voice
he bellowed;
proclaiming that:
every
word
that
we
heard
was
a
lie.
The Stranger's words
woke the dead
and forced us
to come alive.
Making us
open
our eyes.

And we
saw

darkness
proclaiming itself to be light
thinking himself King,
but as our vision cleared
we saw him
as
The Ophidian.

He, The Dragon of old,
architect of the mountain.
The one who profited and made his throne
upon
lost souls,
The one who deceived
The European
with dreams
of imperialism
and distorted the image
of The King.
And used the way as a weapon
to enslave
The African,
and crushed
the nations
hoping to destroy
all human beings
because we
look
like
Adam;
The image of The King.

At The Stranger's voice
all jumped
to their feet.
Then the serpent;
the satan,
Lucifer
opened his mouth
to steal,
kill, and
destroy
all human beings.

He maimed with accusations.
With lies sliced
at thighs.
While the Principalities
appeared behind him
in the sky.
        It was with these tactics
        he created racism
        and fashioned
        the mountain.
        With intent nefarious
        and visions
        of white supremacy
        he hegemonized The European,
        and made them
        his slave
        with hopes to corrupt
        the soul

and make
all humans
animals
through fear and hate.
He rejoiced over
a world enslaved.

Back at the mountain
The Stranger encouraged
us to resist,
but we were
bombarded with
lies that seemed
truer than truth.
As each human
being's lamp flickered
slowly succumbing
to
the darkness.
The Stranger commanded
us to speak
truth.
            What is truth?
            retorted The African.
The Stranger said:
The words of The King
that I taught to you.
So, we spoke to
the mountain.
First as a choir
of whispers.

Then as a multitude
of chants.
       We observed the brightening
       of our lamps.
We became an
army of shouts
loud enough to crack stone
and offered it up as worship
to the true God alone.

A part of the mountain
fell
into the sea
by the words we spoke
to tyranny.
For the first time we observed
fear
on the face
of the enemy.

Every tribe
in every nation
lifted their voices
to sing.
And it was at that moment
that the clouds parted
and
we saw
the face of
The King.

ONE WORD

The King sat on his throne
and spoke
one
word
and vanquished
the serpent
and his servants.

One word,
cracked
the mountain.
Stones came tumbling
down.

One word
laid the path
for the healing
of the nations.
Though slow in motion
I observed
the mountain crumbling.

CRUMBLE

European
you must see
and become
empathy.

Embrace for a moment
the heavy weight
of your ancestry.
Embrace the crushed bodies
scattered across
the centuries
of native people,
stolen land,
and stolen people;
The African,
The Asian,
The Carib,
The Native American.

Feel their sorrow.
Embrace it.
Make it your own.
See through the eye
of the historically oppressed
and massacred
until understanding sheds its light
like the breaking
of the dawn.
Listen
to the song
of The African.

Just listen.

Don't ask.
Don't speak.
Don't seek
justification
nor
vindication.

Listen!

Hold the weight
for a few moments.
Be
silent.
Let understanding wash over you
like a fresh water
spring.
With thought
acknowledge
and deconstruct
systems of oppression.

End the war.

Now lower that heavy weight;
fashioned as a giant stone
from the side
of the mountain.
Lower it slowly
now that full understanding

has turned
to wisdom.
With fresh eyes
opened
drop the weight
at the feet of
The King.

View the mountain
crumbling.

Now forgiven
take your place
with equal inheritance
among the nations.

AT THE KING'S SEAT

Reconcile,
says The King!

To The African,
you are regenerated.

To The European,
you are vindicated.

The King has declared
the work
of satan
undone.
So, African—
so European
choose freedom
together
with The King.

THE KING'S EDICT

Come listen,
says The Stranger.
Listen as The Poet
writes words
of freedom
and peace.

The King
has defeated the serpent,
the dragon, the satan: lucifer,
and his kingdom.
So, none no longer
need to be
slaves to racism
and oppression
anymore.

So, come!
Come, into the 7th day.

Come, to
The African,
The Asian,
The Arab, and
The European!

To all ethnic groups
upon the earth
come!

Come as one

into
freedom
at the feet
of The King.

THE KING SPEAKS

Says The King:
     I speak for myself!

     In my name wicked men
     enslaved The African,
     but
     they
     did not speak
     for me.

     They were wolves
     masquerading
     as my sheep
     sent by the enemy.

     In my name wicked men
     stole land, not their own,
     murdered women, and children,
     but
     they
     did not speak
     for me.

     They were satan's children
     defaming my character
     in an attempt to keep all
     from following me.

     Wicked men are now
     dead men
     facing
     justice
     forever burning.
     Flames for each

of their wicked deeds
and
for rejecting me.

I am the I AM.
I am the giver of peace.
I am The King!
and I speak for myself.
I am the living sacrifice
purchasing all,
so all who believe
are welcome
to be
in my court.
A beautiful tapestry
of all colors
and shades
of human beings
just as I wanted
it to be.

The King [stressed thee; unstressed before a consonant thuh; unstressed before a vowel thee] [king]

Noun

1. God the Father, God the Son, God the Holy Spirit; The One True God.
2. Creator of all things and defender of the weak.
3. The Faithful One.
4. The One who causes all mountains to fall at his feet.

I am Not Ashamed
(The Poet's Epilogue)

I am not a liberal
and
I am not a conservative.

I am a revolutionary
in service
of The King.
I seek the uprooting of society

I am a spiritual being
wrapped in flesh
illuminated
by the Ruach HaKodesh
I can move mountains
and
I can vanquish demons
by the authority
given to me
by The King.

I am an ambassador
invading foreign
territory.
I am a liberator
helping to set
the captive free.
I saw souls come alive
to eternal life.

I am a warrior
and a poet
crafting words given

to me by The King
into luminous
weapons.

I am many things,
but I am
not the I AM.
Save that
title for
The King.

Afterword

I would be remiss if I did not address the realities of the things mentioned at the end of this book. Perhaps when you read this book you felt like The African, in need of something greater than what can be found on this earth. Perhaps you longed in your heart for true peace and to see the face of The King. Although you have this longing perhaps you don't know how to get there. Perhaps like The African you are in need of a stranger to help you find the way. Well allow me; The Poet to become The Stranger for you.

We all face mountains in life. For you, it may not be a mountain of racism and oppression that is at the forefront of your life. Maybe your mountain is an illness that dominates your life, financial troubles, addiction, mental illness, or perhaps it is the greatest mountain of all, the acknowledgment of your own sinfulness.

The first thing you should know is that The King loves you and wishes to tear all your mountains down. Who, is this King? His name is Yeshua Hamashiah; Jesus Christ. Because of the plans of satan and the actions of Adam we human beings, though created as spiritual beings with souls made to live on earth in bodies of flesh, are spiritually dead. Dead because our sinfulness due to Adam being enslaved by satan caused spiritual separation from The King. Why is this important? Well, to be spiritually alive means to live forever even after your body dies, in an everlasting kingdom in the court of The King. To remain spiritually dead means to follow your enslaver; satan to his final destination.

No one needs to follow that path because freedom has already been declared. You see, your King stepped off his throne became a mortal man, walked the perfect righteous path, then gave up his life as an atoning sacrifice for your sin and purchased your freedom. So, like the enslaved Africans after the civil war, but before Juneteenth, you no longer need to live enslaved anymore. Freedom is yours. You only need to take hold of it and make it your own. And how do you make it yours you may ask? Well, it starts first with the self-acknowledgment that you are a sinner, as we all are. Speak to The King, as such:

> LORD, I am a sinner
> enslaved by the enemy,
> but I have a desire to be free.
>
> I acknowledge that you
> purchase my freedom

when you became a man

and died for my sins.

I believe that you rose

from the dead purchasing

my freedom and now

I can have eternal

life.

LORD make me whole.

I seek to follow you

forever.

If you pray a prayer like this I believe that you will be on

your path to freedom but before you conclude this prayer ask the

LORD to fill you with the Ruach HaKodesh; The Holy Spirit.

This is the spirit of Christ; The spirit of God. He is the only one

that can make your spirit come alive.

Now as a resurrected spiritual being live out the

beginning of your eternal life on this earth in your body. Find a

congregation of true believers in Christ and ask to be baptized in

the name of Jesus. Stay with them and grow by the teaching in the word of God; the Holy Bible. Then you will become strong and see your mountains come crashing down. Your spirit and your soul will be sanctified day by day. Then you can take your place with The African who was led by The Stranger to take his stand at the feet of The King.

-Stefon N. Lowman, The Poet

Closing Remarks

In honor of The King
I present this book.
The King; the One true God; Yeshua
Hamashiach;
Jesus Christ

The One who gives me life,
sustains that life,
and causes all the mountains
in my life to come crashing down.
The One who gives me
purpose and peace.

-The Poet

In Memoriam

In loving memory of my friend
Ricky Joharri Gladstone
1980-2005

Because you always believed in me as a writer.
Your name will always live on.

SPECIAL THANKS

Special thanks to my wife, Shayla R. Lowman for editing this book. Thanks to my niecies, Tiffany A. Skeen, Briana Irving, Melissa Romain, my nephew, Joseph Romain, and my brother-in-law, Carlos Romain for helping me with the proofing process. Thanks to my nephew Marc Irving Jr. for inspiring me. I hope these words inspire you. Thank you to my nephew-in-law Ken Skeen for artwork and graphic design consultation.

AUTHOR BIO

Stefon N. Lowman is an American poet born in Brooklyn, NY and raised in North Jamaica Queens, NY by West Indian parents. Both of his parents were born in Saint Vincent and the Grenadines and grew up in Trinidad and Tobago. He is a first generation American and the youngest of seven children. Lowman began writing poetry at age 16 when challenged by his African American history teacher to write a ballad based on *Mother to Son* by Langston Hughes. This sparked a passion for vivid poetic storytelling.

Lowman attended Florida A&M University (FAMU) where he majored in Journalism/Public Relations and minored in Psychology, earning a BS and graduating Magna Cum Laude in 2002. While at FAMU he served as co-creator and editor of The Creative Mindz; a poetry and art section in the campus newspaper, The FAMUAN. After returning to New York City and working in entertainment marketing at HBO and WEtv for a number of years, he left NYC and relocated to North Carolina where he attended North Carolina Central University (NCCU). There he earned dual Masters degree in Mental Health Counseling and School Counseling. He graduated Summa Cum Laude in 2013. He now serves as lead school counselor at a middle school in North Carolina.